FOR HEIDE HELENE

The translation of this story was made from the text appearing in the 1812 edition of Jacob and Wilhelm Grimm's book *Kinde-und Hausmärchen* (*Children's and Household Tales*).

Copyright © 1989, 2013 by NordSüd Verlag AG, CH-8005 Zürich, Switzerland.
First published in Switzerland in 1989 under the title *Der Froschkönig*.
English translation copyright © 1989 by Naomi Lewis

First published in the United States, Great Britain, Canada, Australia, and New Zealand in 1989 by NorthSouth Books Inc., an imprint of NordSüd Verlag AG, CH-8005 Zürich, Switzerland. Distributed in the United States by NorthSouth Books Inc., New York 10016. This edition reissued by NorthSouth Books in 2013.
Library of Congress Cataloging-in-Publication Data is available.
ISBN: 978-0-7358-4140-6
3 5 7 9 • 10 8 6 4 2
Printed in Grafisches Centrum Cuno GmbH & Co. KG,
Calbe, Germany, May 2013.

www.northsouth.com

Printed with all natural paper.

The
Frog Prince
OR IRON HENRY

BY
Jacob & Wilhelm Grimm

ILLUSTRATED BY
Binette Schroeder

TRANSLATED BY
Naomi Lewis

Once, in olden times, when wishes still had power, there lived a king. All of his daughters were beautiful, but the youngest was the loveliest of all. The sun itself, which sees so much, was dazzled when its light shone on her face.

Close to the king's castle was a great dark forest. In that forest, under an ancient lime tree, was a well.

Often, on hot summer days, the king's youngest daughter would wander into the forest and sit down on the edge of the cool well. Then, to pass the time, she would play with a golden ball, throwing it into the air and catching it again. She loved this toy; it was her special treasure. But one day she failed to catch the ball when it fell. It hit the ground, then bounced straight into the water.

The princess gazed down into the depths, but the ball had quite disappeared. The well was so dark and deep that you could not tell what lay under the surface. She began to cry; her sobs grew louder and louder, filling the air with noise. She felt as if nothing could comfort her.

Suddenly she heard a voice. "Princess," it said, "whatever is the matter? Your howling could move the heart of a stone!"

Where did the voice come from? She looked around and saw a frog poking his big ugly head out of the water. "So it was you speaking just now, old water-splasher! Why am I crying? I'll tell you. My golden ball fell down the well, and I've lost it now forever."

"I can help you," said the frog. "But what will you give me if I bring back your plaything?" "Whatever you want, dear frog." said the princess. "My finest clothes, my jewels, even my golden crown."

"Oh, I don't want clothes and jewels, things of that kind," said the frog. "But I would like some love and affection. Now, if you promise to let me be your special friend and playmate, if you let me sit beside you at the dinner table, eat from your golden cup and sleep in your little bed — if you promise me these small things, I will dive down and bring back your golden ball."

"Yes, yes," said the princess, "I'll promise whatever you want if only you bring back my lovely ball." But she thought to herself: The creature is talking nonsense. It's a frog! It lives in the water with frogs. How can it come to court and behave as if it were human? The frog, though, heard only the promise. He nodded, then dived down into the well. After a while he swam to the surface with the golden ball in his mouth and shook it out onto the grass.

The princess was overjoyed
to see her treasure again. She
picked it up and rushed away.
"Wait! Wait!" cried the frog;
"I can't run at that speed!
Your legs are longer than mine."
But his croaking calls were
wasted. The princess raced on,
reached the castle, and put
the frog out of her mind. The
poor fellow turned sadly and
went back into the well.

The next day the princess sat down in her usual place at the royal dinner table. She was about to take a cherry from her golden plate when she heard a peculiar noise — *splosh, splosh, flop, flop* — on the marble stairs. Something was crawling up, step-by-step. That something reached the door and stopped. It knocked: *thud, thud*. It spoke in a croaking voice. "King's daughter," it said, "open the door!"

Fearfully the princess went to the door and peered outside. There was the frog, patiently waiting. She shut the door and quickly went back to her place at the table. Oh, she was afraid.

She sat quite still, but her heart beat fast — so fast that her father noticed. "Child," he said, "what is the matter? Is an ogre waiting outside to carry you off?" "No, no," she said. "It isn't an ogre; it's a nasty frog." "A frog? What does he want?" "Dear father, as I was playing by the well, my golden ball fell into the water. I was crying so hard that the frog offered to bring it back. Only he made me promise to let him be my playmate and sit next to me at the table. I never thought that he could leave the well and come to the palace. Now he is outside and wants to come in!" At that moment the knocking started again. *Thud, thud! Thud, thud!* And the listeners at the table heard these words:

There was a princess.
Open the door!
She made me a promise,
I'll tell you more!
A promise, a promise
That she must keep.
I've come for food and drink
and sleep.
Princess, O Princess, you
cannot hide!
Your frog companion waits outside!

"Daughter," said the king. "You made a promise; it must be kept. Go and open the door."

Slowly the princess did as she was told. At once the frog hopped in and followed her footsteps to her chair.

Then he called out. "Lift me up!"

"Do as he says," the king commanded. But as soon as she had put the frog on the chair, he leapt onto the table. "Move your golden plate nearer," he croaked, "and we can eat together."

The princess moved the plate, but it was easy to see that she was none too happy. The frog enjoyed the dinner — but what about the princess? Every morsel stuck in the poor girl's throat.

At last the frog finished his meal and spoke again.

"I have eaten all I want," he said. "Now I am tired. Kindly carry me to your room, put me in your silken bed, and we can go to sleep."

The king's daughter began to cry. She was really afraid of the frog, so cold to the touch — and now he wanted to sleep in her beautiful, clean bed.

But the king frowned and said sternly, "If someone has helped you in time of need, you must not scorn him when this need has gone."

What could she do? She picked up the frog between finger and thumb, carried him upstairs, and put him in a corner.

She waited a little while then went to bed.

But no sooner was her head on the pillow than she heard the frog creeping along the floor. "I am tired," he said. "I want to sleep comfortably, just as you do."

"Now pick me up, or I shall tell your father."

The princess was enraged, but she dared not refuse.

She picked up the frog and then — with a rush of anger — threw him with all her might against the wall.

As she did so, she cried out: "Now are you satisfied, you nasty creature?"

But even while he fell, an astonishing thing happened. The frog began to change his shape; he was a frog no longer but a young and handsome prince, gazing at her with eyes that were both beautiful and kind.

THE KING REJOICED AT THE
NEWS. HE WELCOMED THE PRINCE
AS A HUSBAND FOR HIS DEAR
DAUGHTER. AND SO THE TWO WERE
MARRIED. THE PRINCE HAD A STRANGE
TALE TO TELL. A WICKED WITCH HAD CAST
A SPELL ON HIM. A SPELL THAT ONLY THE
LOVELIEST PRINCESS COULD BREAK. NOW HE
WAS FREE! "TOMORROW," HE SAID. "WE SHALL
TRAVEL TO MY KINGDOM." THEN THEY FELL ASLEEP.

When the morning came, they were wakened by the sun. They saw that a carriage was waiting at the gates. It was drawn by eight white horses, with white ostrich plumes on their heads and trappings of all gold. At the back stood a serving man with three iron bands around his heart. So great had been the man's grief when his master was bewitched that he had placed the three bands around him to keep his heart from breaking.

"My faithful Henry!" said the prince, and greeted him joyfully.

And now the bride and bridegroom
were ready to leave for the
young man's own kingdom.
Faithful Henry lifted each one
into the carriage, then took his place
behind them.

After they had driven a short
distance, a sharp crack was heard.
Startled, the bridegroom spoke:
Henry, Henry, what's that sound?
Is the carriage breaking?

No, Sire, 'tis a ring that bound
My heart when it was aching.
But now my lord is freed and back,
Joy has made the iron crack.

Then a second time they heard
a crack, and a third time after
that. Each time the prince feared
that the carriage was breaking.
But no — the sound came from the
last of the bands freeing faithful
Henry's heart.

Grief forged the bonds at first,
Grief for his lord accurst.
Joy made the bonds to burst.